THE
Baby's
Bedtime Book

KAY CHORAO

E. P. Dutton   New York

The author and publisher gratefully acknowledge permission to reprint on:
    pages 46 & 47, "Cradle-Song" from *The Sceptred Flute* by Sarojini Naidu, published by Dodd, Mead & Company, Inc.
    page 48, "The White Seal's Lullaby" from the story "The White Seal" by Rudyard Kipling in *Rudyard Kipling's Verse: Definitive Edition.* Used by permission of The National Trust; MacMillan London, Limited; and Doubleday & Company, Inc.

The author and publisher believe that the necessary permissions from publishers, authors, and authorized agents have been obtained. In the event any questions arise as to the use of any material, the author and publisher express regret for any error unconsciously made and will be pleased to make the necessary corrections in future editions of this book.

Library of Congress Cataloging in Publication Data
Chorao, Kay.
    The baby's bedtime book.

    Includes index.
    Summary: Presents twenty-seven traditional rhymes, poems, and lullabies for bedtime from a variety of sources.
    1. Children's poetry.   2. Nursery rhymes.
[1. Nursery rhymes.   2. Lullabies.
3. Poetry—Collections.   4. Bedtime—Poetry]
I. Title.
PN6109.97.C48   1984   808.81   84-6067
ISBN 0-525-44149-2

Published in the United States by E. P. Dutton,
a division of Penguin Books USA Inc.

Published simultaneously in Canada by
Fitzhenry & Whiteside Limited, Toronto
Editor: Ann Durell   Designer: Riki Levinson

Printed in Mexico

This book belongs to

_____

Contents

Dance, Little Baby

Dance, little baby, dance up high.
Never mind, baby, mother is by.
Crow and caper, caper and crow;
There, little baby, there you go
Up to the ceiling, down to the ground,
Backwards and forwards, round and round.
Dance, little baby, and mother will sing
With the merry coral, ding, ding, ding!

Stars

I'm glad the stars are over me
And not beneath my feet,
Where we should trample on them
Like cobbles on the street.
I think it is a happy thing
That they are set so far;
It's best to have to look up high
When you would see a star.

Tree Shadows

All hushed the trees are waiting
On tiptoe for the sight
Of moonrise shedding splendor
Across the dusk of night.
Ah, now the moon is risen
And lo, without a sound
The trees all write their welcome
Far along the ground!

(from the Japanese)

Night

by William Blake

The sun descending in the west
The evening star does shine;
The birds are silent in their nest,
And I must seek for mine.

The moon like a flower
In heaven's high bower,
With silent delight,
Sits and smiles on the night.

At Night

by Anne Blackwell Payne

When I go to bed at night,
The darkness is a bear.
He crouches in the corner
Or hides behind a chair;
The one who tells me stories—
She does not know he's there.

But when she kisses me good-night,
And darkness starts to creep
Across the floor, why, then I see
It's just a woolly sheep
That nibbles at my rugs awhile
Before we go to sleep.

Girls and Boys, Come Out To Play

Girls and boys, come out to play;

The moon doth shine as bright as day;

Leave your supper and leave your sleep,

And come with your playfellows into the street.

Come with a whoop, come with a call,

Come with a goodwill, or come not at all.

Up the ladder and down the wall,

A halfpenny roll will serve us all.

You find milk, and I'll find flour,

And we'll have pudding in half an hour.

My Bed Is a Boat

by Robert Louis Stevenson

My bed is like a little boat;
    Nurse helps me in when I embark;
She girds me in my sailor's coat
    And starts me in the dark.

At night, I go on board and say
    Good night to all my friends on shore;
I shut my eyes and sail away
    And see and hear no more.

And sometimes things to bed I take,
    As prudent sailors have to do;
Perhaps a slice of wedding cake,
    Perhaps a toy or two.

All night across the dark we steer;
    But when the day returns at last,
Safe in my room, beside the pier,
    I find my vessel fast.

Hush, Little Baby

Hush, little baby, don't say a word,
Papa's gonna buy you a mockingbird.
If that mockingbird won't sing,
Papa's gonna buy you a diamond ring.

If that diamond ring turns brass,
Papa's gonna buy you a looking glass.
If that looking glass gets broke,
Papa's gonna buy you a billy goat.

If that billy goat won't pull,

Papa's gonna buy you a cart and bull.

If that cart and bull turn over,

Papa's gonna buy you a dog named Rover.

If that dog named Rover won't bark,

Papa's gonna buy you a horse and cart.

If that horse and cart fall down,

You'll still be the sweetest baby in town.

Twinkle, Twinkle, Little Star

by Jane Taylor

Twinkle, twinkle, little star,
How I wonder what you are!
Up above the world so high,
Like a diamond in the sky.

When the blazing sun is gone,
When he nothing shines upon,
Then you show your little light,
Twinkle, twinkle, all the night.

Then the traveler in the dark
Thanks you for your tiny spark;
He could not see which way to go,
If you did not twinkle so.

In the dark blue sky you keep
And often through my curtains peep,
For you never shut your eye
Till the sun is in the sky.

As your bright and tiny spark
Lights the traveler in the dark,
Though I know not what you are,
Twinkle, twinkle, little star.

I See the Moon

I see the moon,
And the moon sees me;
God bless the moon,
And God bless me.

Rock-a-bye, Baby

Rock-a-bye, baby,
   On the tree-top,
When the wind blows,
   The cradle will rock;
When the bough breaks,
   The cradle will fall,
And down will come baby,
   Cradle and all.

All the Pretty Horses

Hushaby,

Don't you cry.

Go to sleep, my little baby.

When you wake, you shall have

All the pretty little horses.

Blacks

And bays,

Dapples

And grays.

All the pretty little horses.

Hushaby,

Don't you cry.

Go to sleep, my little baby.

How They Sleep

Some things go to sleep in such a funny way:

Little birds stand on one leg and tuck their heads away.

Chickens do the same, standing on their perch;

Little mice lie soft and still as if they were in church.

Kittens curl up close, in such a funny ball;

Horses hang their sleepy heads and stand still in a stall.

Sometimes dogs stretch out or curl up in a heap;
Cows lie down upon their sides when they go to sleep.
But little babies dear are snugly tucked in beds,
Warm with blankets, all so soft, and pillows for their heads.
Bird and beast and babe—I wonder which of all—
Dream the dearest dreams that down from dreamland fall!

Minnie and Winnie

by Alfred, Lord Tennyson

Minnie and Winnie
Slept in a shell.
Sleep, little ladies!
And they slept well.

Pink was the shell within,
Silver without;
Sounds of the great sea
Wandered about.

Sleep, little ladies!
Wake not soon!
Echo on echo
Dies to the moon.

Two bright stars
Peeped into the shell.
"What are they dreaming of?
Who can tell?"

Startled a green linnet
Out of the croft;
Wake, little ladies!
The sun is aloft.

A Chill

by Christina Rossetti

What can lambkins do
All the keen night through?
Nestle by their woolly mother,
The careful ewe.

What can nestlings do
In the nightly dew?
Sleep beneath their mother's wing
Till day breaks anew.

If in field or tree,
There might only be
Such a warm soft sleepy place
Found for me!

Good Night

by Jane Taylor

Little baby, lay your head
On your pretty cradle-bed;
Shut your eye-peeps, now the day
And the light are gone away;
All the clothes are tucked in tight;
Little baby dear, good night.

Yes, my darling, well I know
How the bitter wind doth blow;
And the winter's snow and rain
Patter on the windowpane;
But they cannot come in here,
To my little baby dear;

For the window shutteth fast,
Till the stormy night is past;
And the curtains warm are spread
Round about her cradle-bed.
So till morning shineth bright,
Little baby dear, good night.

39

The Land of Nod

by Robert Louis Stevenson

From breakfast on all through the day
At home among my friends I stay;
But every night I go abroad
Afar into the land of Nod.

All by myself I have to go,
With none to tell me what to do—
All alone beside the streams
And up the mountainsides of dreams.

The strangest things are there for me,
Both things to eat and things to see,
And many frightening sights abroad
Till morning in the land of Nod.

Try as I like to find the way,
I never can get back by day,
Nor can remember plain and clear
The curious music that I hear.

Gaelic Lullaby

Hush! the waves are rolling in,
    White with foam, white with foam;
Father toils amid the din;
    But baby sleeps at home.

Hush! the winds roar hoarse and deep,
    On they come, on they come!
Brother seeks the wandering sheep;
    But baby sleeps at home.

Hush! the rain sweeps over the knowes,
    Where they roam, where they roam;
Sister goes to seek the cows;
    But baby sleeps at home.

Lullaby and Good Night

Lullaby and good night,
With roses bedight,
With lilies bespread,
Is baby's wee bed.
Lay thee down now and rest,
May thy slumber be blest.

Lullaby and good night,
Thy mother's delight;
Bright angels around
My darling shall stand;
They will guard thee from harm;
Thou shalt wake in my arms.

(from the German)

Cradle-Song

by Sarojini Naidu

From groves of spice,
O'er fields of rice,
Athwart the lotus-stream,
I bring for you,
Aglint with dew,
A little lovely dream.

Sweet, shut your eyes,
The wild fire-flies
Dance through the fairy *neem*;
From the poppy-bole
For you I stole
A little lovely dream.

Dear eyes, good-night,
In golden light
The stars around you gleam;
On you I press
With soft caress
A little lovely dream.

The White Seal's Lullaby

by Rudyard Kipling

Oh! hush thee, my baby, the night is behind us,
　　And black are the waters that sparkled so green.
The moon, o'er the combers, looks downward to find us
　　At rest in the hollows that rustle between.
Where billow meets billow, then soft be thy pillow;
　　Ah, weary wee flipperling, curl at thy ease!
The storm shall not wake thee, nor shark overtake thee,
　　Asleep in the arms of the slow-swinging seas.

Sleep, Baby, Sleep!

Sleep, baby, sleep!
Thy father watches the sheep.
Thy mother is shaking the dreamland tree,
And down falls a little dream on thee.
Sleep, baby, sleep!

Sleep, baby, sleep!
The large stars are the sheep.
The little stars are the lambs, I guess,
The big round moon is the shepherdess.
Sleep, baby, sleep!

Sweet and Low

by Alfred, Lord Tennyson

Sweet and low, sweet and low,
   Wind of the western sea,
Low, low, breathe and blow,
   Wind of the western sea!
Over the rolling waters go,
Come from the dying moon, and blow,
   Blow him again to me
While my little one, while my pretty one
   Sleeps.

Sleep and rest, sleep and rest,
   Father will come to thee soon;
Rest, rest, on mother's breast,
   Father will come to thee soon;
Father will come to his babe in the nest,
Silver sails all out of the west
   Under the silver moon.
Sleep, my little one, sleep, my pretty one,
   Sleep.

Safe in Bed

Matthew, Mark, Luke and John,
Bless the bed that I lie on!
Four corners to my bed,
Five angels there lie spread:
    Two at my head,
    Two at my feet,
One at my heart, my soul to keep.

All Through the Night

by Sir Harold Boulton

Sleep, my child, and peace attend thee
All through the night.
Guardian angels God will send thee
All through the night.
Soft the drowsy hours are creeping,
Hill and vale in slumber sleeping,
I my loving vigil keeping
All through the night.

While the moon her watch is keeping
All through the night;
While the weary world is sleeping
All through the night;
O'er thy spirit gently stealing,
Visions of delight revealing,
Breathes a pure and holy feeling
All through the night.

Now I Lay Me Down To Sleep

Now I lay me down to sleep,
I pray thee, Lord, my soul to keep;
Thy love go with me all the night
And wake me with the morning light.

Day Is Done

Day is done,
Gone the sun—
From the earth,
From the hills,
From the sky.
All is well,
Safely rest.
God is nigh.

Index of first lines